A Donkey's Little Tale

R. Mitchell Scott

Illustrated by Brittany Huskey

Ambassador International
GREENVILLE, SOUTH CAROLINA & BELFAST, NORTHERN IRELAND

www.ambassador-international.com

A Donkey's Little Tale

Illustrated by Brittany Huskey

ISBN: 978-1-62020-261-6
eISBN: 978-1-62020-362-0

Cover Design & Page Layout: Hannah Nichols
Ebook Conversion: Anna Riebe

AMBASSADOR INTERNATIONAL
Emerald House
427 Wade Hampton Blvd
Greenville, SC 29609, USA
www.ambassador-international.com

AMBASSADOR BOOKS
The Mount
2 Woodstock Link
Belfast, BT6 8DD, Northern Ireland, UK
www.ambassador-international.com

The colophon is a trademark of Ambassador

Dedication
To Cathy and John Rogert

Friends like these are the kind that Jesus wants us to be. Rare is the opportunity to witness a sacrificial commitment and meticulous devotion to a promise without fail. Their faithfulness in prayer and help during my time of need never faltered. Allegiance to their word honored both the Lord and me. Their friendship, sacrifice and love will always remain a cherished gift. Well done, thou good and faithful servants.

Acknowledgements

I would be a terrible daughter and sister if I failed to honor my mother, Thelma Lesher Mitchell and my father, the late Stanley Ross Mitchell. The genetic makeup of their union produced five artisans, each possessing multiple gifts and talents. I must personally commend my mother for cleaning up every mess I left after my artistic endeavors, and I thank the Lord for a Daddy who studied the Scriptures, bringing the stories alive at home and then at church, where we ultimately came to know God.

While walking through the wilderness one dry and thirsty day, my master led me to a small oasis 'long the way.

$\mathcal{H}$e tied my reins so neatly to a waving royal palm,
then stroked my soft brown mane and fairly bade me to be calm.

$\mathcal{I}$ braced the coolness of the breeze and tarried in the shade.
I saw the master by the pool and to him loudly brayed.

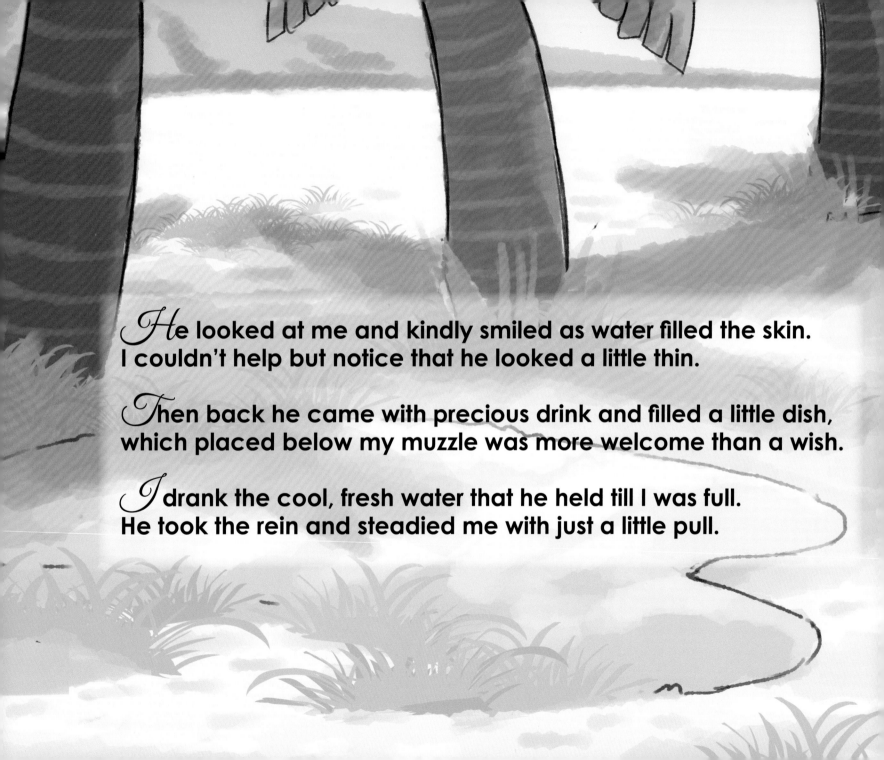

He looked at me and kindly smiled as water filled the skin.
I couldn't help but notice that he looked a little thin.

Then back he came with precious drink and filled a little dish,
which placed below my muzzle was more welcome than a wish.

I drank the cool, fresh water that he held till I was full.
He took the rein and steadied me with just a little pull.

Then turned he to my passenger still resting on my back.
She handed down her cloak and shawl and then a little pack.

The master stooped and laid her things o'er fronds upon the sands,
then lifted up to her a pair of rough and leathered hands.

Her hands went to his shoulders as she looked into his face,
and master gently eased her down into a soft embrace.

The lady took her garments up and laid them 'cross my back,
then kneeling to the sandy ground picked up the tiny pack.

The master and his lady walked together hand in hand.
Once more he knelt to fill the skin from water in the sand.

She drank the cool refreshment, quiet breeze the only sound.
I saw from such short distance that her form was very round.

Without a word they walked along, returning to my side.
Her motherhood impending was impossible to hide.

The master took her garments down and shook out every fold,
then bundled them around her to protect her from the cold.

She placed the little package in the master's loving hand.
He stooped and laid it gingerly upon the cool white sand.

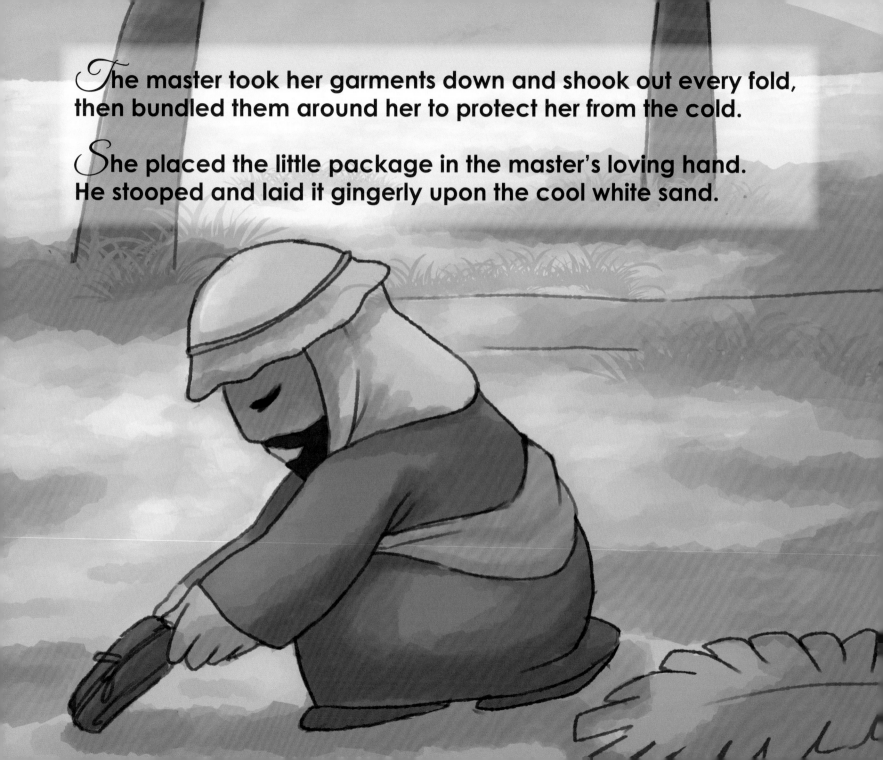

His strong arms lifted up with ease the little mother fair.
He set her squarely on my back and softly stroked her hair.

One quiet tear rolled down his cheek; his eyes were full of love.
He handed her the little pack, then turned his face above.

He closed his eyes, no words he spoke, though lips did gently smile.
The master seemed to sense that joy would come in just a while.

My rein was loosed, and off we set, the little town in view.
A few more miles—a good night's rest—the journey nearly through.

At city's gate, the news was clear. No rooms were left to rent.
The farthest corner of the town was where we all were sent.

We wove through streets of cobblestone, past fragrant marketplace.
The dread of lowly tenement was etched on master's face.

Then suddenly, before my eyes—a stable by a stream.
No better spot imaginable—not in my fondest dream!

Contented cattle lowing soft in warmth of gated stall,
another donkey just like me stood quiet by the wall.

A manger overflowed with hay, the air was moist and warm.
The ox and lamb slept peacefully, no fear of pain or harm.

More perfect place was ne'er prepared for journey's needed rest.
How wonderful that master found for us the very best!

Once more the master gently set his bride upon the floor.
She looked around as if she knew we could not ask for more.

The gentle mother spread her cloak across the manger hay,
Then wrapping tightly in her shawl, she humbly knelt to pray.

She clutched the little package tight, then placed it on her bed.
I wondered what this thing must be, wrapped in its linen thread.

I nestled in a cozy spot; I could not fight the sleep.
I dreamt of quiet meadows full of woolly, grazing sheep.

I suddenly was wakened by a brilliant, starry light.
It beamed through tiny windows after shattering the night!

The manger bed appeared to glow with light and silence deep.
The star shone on a swaddled form—a tiny babe asleep!

I wondered who this child could be—must be an heir to grace.
Who but the sons of greatest chiefs would merit such a place?

*T*he mother mild took up the pack she'd fashioned, bound, and blessed.
Unwrapping it so tenderly, she held it to her breast.

Then slowly rising near the hay that served as baby's bed,
she placed a tiny pillow underneath his little head.

'Twas in this quiet moment when a golden bell did ring,
I realized my honored place in service to a King!

How marvelous! How wonderful! For I must surely be
the luckiest donkey in the world—I'm thankful to be me!

"A Donkey's Little Tale" was a Divine gift on the morning of December 28, 2004. I, the "author," R. Mitchell Scott, sat down with coffee and Bible. Throughout the month my devotional time teemed with spirit-charged poetic energy. Scripture fairly demanded a creative outpouring.

Reading the brief accounts of Matthew 1 and Luke 2, the passages wanted for detail regarding the short journey to Bethlehem made by Joseph and Mary. Pondering the scriptural gaps, I was disappointed by the few and brief biblical accounts glaringly deplete of intimate detail. The couple blended in among the throng making their way to Bethlehem to register for the census. Was there no one to chronicle the intimate details of the love story between the chosen parents of the Son of God? I had questions but no one to ask . . . except the Lord. Suddenly, inspiration! Did they bring a donkey? If so, what might he have seen or heard? The child in me captured my thoughts. I had no one to ask, so I asked the Lord—what did the donkey see? Three hours later the breathtaking poetic contemplations were etched in a spiral notebook courtesy of my trusty yellow #2 pencil and the gracious hand of God.

"A Donkey's Little Tale" turned out to be the crowning glory of my poetic bonanza, and it has been protected at all costs. Very few have read it over the past decade, and those who have, whisked away tears at the end. My beautiful sister, Lana, the first to hear a reading of "A Donkey's Little Tale," has faithfully nagged me for these ten-plus years to get on with the publishing. Now, here it is. Glory to God!

I was provided several pounds of Lizella clay in a sculpture class in college. The instructor was thrilled by the life-like quality of the clay. It sat unused in my garage for many years until I finally had time and energy to think about pottery. When the inspiration for A Donkey's Little Tale came in 2004, I had not the time or energy to get it published. Meantime, I puttered in the garage from time to time and had fashioned a small herd of horses, turtles, ocarinas and dogs, using a variety of craft clays and glazes. My relatives snatched them up. After a decade, the A Donkey's Little Tale manuscript was still in a box. Circumstances changed and my sister's nagging finally took root and the Lord brought two writers into my world-- Ruth Ellinger and Deborah Coty to mentor me. I joined Brandon Christian Writers and read A Donkey's Little Tale to the group. I also attended several Florida Inspirational Writer's Retreat events. One Christmas, I crafted a Nativity crèche out of scrap clay. It was so cute, I sent it to my brother as a Christmas gift. He still puts it out every year. I made lots of different sizes and styles of crèches and gifted them, mostly to family on holidays. I wanted one for me, so I got out my dried hump of Lizella clay and was truly amazed by its life-like qualities. I knew then I wanted to illustrate ADLT. I wanted to illustrate the book, but I did not want to draw it. My husband drove me to Lizella, Georgia, where the one and only backyard clay pit still provides artisans with the lively, clay that practically molds itself and fires to a gorgeous red bisque. We bought 300 pounds, and I look forward to more projects.